ya...ing

...ng

smelling

petting

giving

washing

writing

For Mark

First U.S. edition 1993
First published in Great Britain in 1993 by Walker Books Ltd., London.

Library of Congress Cataloging-in-Publication Data:

Hughes, Shirley.
Giving / Shirley Hughes.—1st U.S. ed.
Summary: A little girl and her baby brother experience the
various aspects of giving, finding that it is nice whether you are
giving a present, a smile, or a kiss.
[1. Generosity—Fiction. 2. Gifts—Fiction.] I. Title.
PZ7.H87395G1   1993   92-53002
[E]—dc20

ISBN 1-56402-129-7

10 9 8 7 6 5 4 3 2 1

Printed and bound in Hong Kong
by Dai Nippon Printing Co. (H.K.) Ltd.

The artwork for this book was done with colored pencils,
watercolors, and pen line.

Candlewick Press
2067 Massachusetts Avenue
Cambridge, Massachusetts 02140

Giving

Shirley Hughes

CANDLEWICK PRESS
CAMBRIDGE, MASSACHUSETTS

I gave Mom a present on her birthday,
all wrapped up in pretty paper.

And she gave me a big kiss.

I gave Dad a very special picture
that I painted at play group.

And he gave me a ride on his shoulders most of the way home.

I gave the baby some
slices of my apple.

We ate them sitting under the table.

At dinnertime the baby gave me
two of his soggy bread crusts.

That wasn't much of a present!

You can give
someone an
angry look ...

or a big smile!

You can give a tea party...

or a seat on a crowded bus.

On my birthday Grandma and Grandpa
gave me a beautiful doll carriage.
I said "Thank you," and gave
them each a big hug.

And I gave my dear Bemily
a ride in it, all the way down the
garden path and back again.

I tried to give the
cat a ride too,

but she gave me a
nasty scratch!

So Dad had to give my poor arm
a kiss and a Band-Aid.

Sometimes, just when
I've built a big castle
out of blocks,

the baby comes along and
gives it a big swipe!
And it all falls down.

Then I feel like giving
the baby a big
swipe too.

But I don't, because

he *is* my baby brother, after all.

sleeping

dancing

crying

waving

giving

eating

skipping

telling

listening

thinking